For Mum, Dad and Penny with love
- L.G.

For Paul and Clare
- C.S.

For Rachael and Rolo
- B.O'D.

Text copyright © 2007 Lauren Graham
Illustrations copyright © 2007 Chris Stephens

First published in Ireland by O'Donnell Press 2007
12 Coolemoyne Park, Jordanstown, Co. Antrim BT37 0RP
Telephone: 028 9096 6493
Email: b.odonnell93@ntlworld.com
www.odonnellpress.com

Special thanks to Exploris, Portaferry.

A CIP catalogue record of this book is available from the British Library.

Printed in Ireland by GPS Colour Graphics Ltd.
Repro scanning by iris colour.

ISBN 978-0-9553325-2-4

1 2 3 4 5 6 7 8 9 10

O'DONNELL PRESS

Scrabo
the Strangford Seal

By Lauren Graham
Illustrated by Chris Stephens

Scrabo the seal pup lived with his mother in a beautiful part of Ireland called Strangford Lough. From nearly the moment that he was born, he was able to swim. He loved nothing better than gliding through the shallow water, using his large hind flippers.

Scrabo the Strangford Seal belongs to:

_____

_____

Scrabo's mother was protective of her little son. She swam nearby at all times, watching him as he explored his new surroundings. Then, when he began to get tired, she led him out of the water for a rest on the warm, sun-baked rocks on the shores of Strangford Lough. As they lay together, basking in the splendid summer sunshine, she talked gently to her little boy, telling him about her wonderful adventures in the lough and warning little Scrabo about its dangers.

"Scrabo my dear," she cautioned, "You must stay in the shallow water, close to the shore. Don't swim into the deep water until you are older. In the middle of the lough there are rushing tidal waters called The Narrows. The current in this part of the lough is too strong for a seal pup. Stay near the shore where you will be safe."

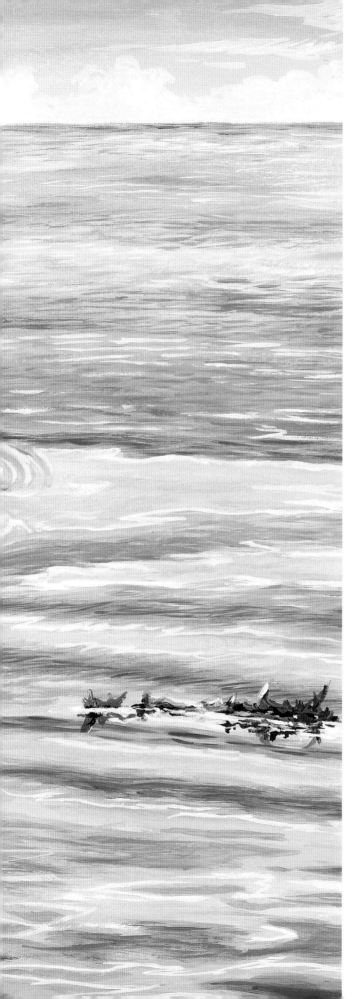

Scrabo loved his mother very much and listened carefully to what she said, but like all seal pups, Scrabo was curious.
As the days went by, he swam further and further out from the shore and he explored further and further around the coast.
All the time, his mother watched him from a short distance away, making sure that he was always safely within her sight.

One day, Scrabo swam around the coast until he came to a picture postcard place called Portaferry. He swam close to the shore, watching the buzz of activity on land. Cars were lined behind one another in an orderly queue to drive onto a big boat. Scrabo's mother swam up beside him. "That's the Strangford ferry," she explained. "It brings people and cars across to the other side of the lough. Let's swim over to those nearby rocks and you can watch the ferry sail." Without another word, Scrabo's mother manoeuvred him onto the rocky shore. Then she stretched herself out and started to gossip to the other seals.

As the ferry left the port, Scrabo slipped unseen into the still water. Excitedly he swam close to the ferry, following its foamy trail. By the time his mother had realised he was missing, Scrabo was swimming through the deep waters in the middle of Strangford Lough.

Scrabo was very excited.
"What an adventure!"
he thought to himself.

Suddenly, he felt the water
tugging him downwards.
The current swirled him round
and round. It pulled him down
and down. He could feel
himself being dragged deeper
and deeper into the dark,
murky waters below.

As he struggled to swim to the surface, strong seaweed caught around his flippers. Poor Scrabo was stuck in its slippery hold. Normally Scrabo only stayed below the surface of the water for five or ten minutes at a time, but now he was caught underwater and couldn't get free.

He began to panic and longed to be back in the protective care of his loving mother. Why had he not listened to her? She had warned him about the tidal waters in the middle of the lough. Why had he been so silly and swum away from the safety of the shore? He tugged and tugged at the seaweed, trying to get free but the more that he twisted and turned, the more he became tangled in the seaweed's strong grip.

In a last attempt for freedom, Scrabo pulled at the seaweed for all he was worth. It tore from the rocks below and Scrabo swam frantically to the surface of the water. Gasping for breath, he floated helplessly. He was too exhausted to swim to the shore so he just lay there, drifting with the tide. He closed his eyes and thought of his mother.

Early the next morning, a caring lady and her little black dog found Scrabo lying weak and powerless on the beach. Poor Scrabo had a large cut on his left side and he was unable to move. The lady phoned the Exploris seal sanctuary and they swung quickly into action in an effort to rescue the injured seal pup.

Scrabo was immediately brought back to the seal sanctuary where he was weighed and a vet tended to his injury. Then he was left on his own in a big pen. For the first few days, he was tube-fed with a fish mixture. However, it didn't take long before he was eating whole herrings and when his cut had healed and he felt much better, he was moved to the outdoor nursery pond. It was lovely to mix with other seals again. It made him think about his mother and how much he missed being in her loving care.

By now, Scrabo's rescuers knew that it was nearly time for him to be released. They put him into a big pond to prepare him for returning to the wild. On the day of his release, Scrabo was wrapped in a net, lifted from the pond and put into a huge plastic bucket. Then he was tipped out onto the beach. He knew that he had been freed to return again to Strangford Lough and he had no intention of waiting around. He wriggled into the water as quickly as he could and swam away in search of his mother.

It was wonderful to be gliding once more through the waters of Strangford Lough. Scrabo didn't have to search for long before he found his mother. She was overjoyed to see her darling boy once more. She swam protectively beside him, lovingly watching to make sure that no harm would come again to her little Scrabo, the Strangford seal.

Enjoy more great picture books from
O'Donnell Press

ISBN 0-9553325-1-6   ISBN 0-9553325-0-8   ISBN 0-9546163-5-9

ISBN 0-9546163-7-5   ISBN 0-9546163-1-6   ISBN 0-9546163-6-7

www.odonnellpress.com